Special Days
with
Honey
and Bear

Stories by
URSULA DUBOSARSKY

Pictures by
RON BROOKS

PUFFIN BOOKS

For Gabrielle Meagher, with love and thanks.   U.D.

For Ursula, and for Jane . . . for their patience.   R.B.

Puffin Books

Published by the Penguin Group
Penguin Books Australia Ltd
250 Camberwell Road,
Camberwell, Victoria 3124, Australia
Penguin Books Ltd
80 Strand, London WC2R 0RL, England
Penguin Putnam Inc.
375 Hudson Street, New York, New York 10014, USA
Penguin Books, a division of Pearson Canada
10 Alcorn Avenue, Toronto, Ontario, Canada M4V 3B2
Penguin Books (NZ) Ltd
Cnr Rosedale and Airborne Roads, Albany, Auckland, New Zealand
Penguin Books (South Africa) (Pty) Ltd
24 Sturdee Avenue, Rosebank, Johannesburg 2196, South Africa
Penguin Books India (P) Ltd
11, Community Centre, Panchsheel Park, New Delhi 110 017, India

First published by Penguin Books Australia, 2002
10 9 8 7 6 5 4 3 2
Copyright © Ursula Dubosarsky, 2002
Illustrations copyright © Ron Brooks, 2002

Typeset in 18/32pt Cochin
Printed in China by Everberst Printing Co Ltd
Designed by Ron Brooks

National Library of Australia
Cataloguing-in-Publication data:

Dubosarsky, Ursula, 1961– .
Special days with Honey and Bear
014 130630 0

1. Brooks, Ron, 1948 - . II. Title.
A823.3

www.puffin.com.au

Contents

Staying Up Late   4

The Mirror   14

Bear's Birthday   22

Bear Gets Lost   32

Honey's Dream   42

Staying Up Late

Honey and Bear were sitting in the kitchen eating apples.

'Bear,' said Honey, 'today is a very special day.'

'Is it?' said Bear, his mouth full.

'Yes,' said Honey. 'Today is the last day of the year.'

'Oh,' said Bear.

'So do you know what we have to do tonight?' said Honey.

'What?' asked Bear, excited.

'We have to stay up till the middle of the night and look at the clock,' said Honey.

'That doesn't sound very interesting,'
said Bear.

'But it is, Bear,' said Honey. 'We will look
at the clock, and when both hands are on the
twelve, it will be the New Year! Then we
will give each other a kiss.'

Bear thought for a moment. 'I could give
you a kiss now,' he suggested, 'in case I am
too tired in the middle of the night.'

'No, Bear,' said Honey. 'We have to wait
until twelve o'clock.'

When they had finished the apples,
Honey and Bear went outside. They went
for a long, long walk by the lake until the
sun was setting.

By the time they got home, it was night.

Bear sat in his armchair and looked at
the clock.

Nine o'clock. He yawned. He was already
tired. How would he stay up until twelve
o'clock?

'Let's do a jigsaw,' said Honey.

So they sat on the floor and began a jigsaw.
It was hard. After a while, Bear stood up and
looked at the clock. Ten o'clock.

Oh dear, he thought.

'Bear, can you see where this piece goes?'
asked Honey.

Bear sat down.

The clock ticked.

Bear yawned.

Eleven o'clock.

'Let's go to sleep, Honey,' Bear said.
'Please?'

But Honey was busy with the puzzle.

Bear sighed.

He picked up a piece and tried to fit
it in. But he was just too tired.

At last, Bear couldn't wait any longer.

'Honey,' he said, 'I *have* to go to bed!'

'But Bear! Look! Look at the clock!' Honey shouted, flapping her wings.

Bear looked.

The little hand was on the twelve, and the big hand was nearly there.

'It's almost the New Year!' said Bear.

Honey and Bear held their breath.

They waited. They watched.

The big hand moved such a tiny bit and –

'HAPPY NEW YEAR!' cried Honey and Bear at the same time. They forgot all about the puzzle, and gave each other a big kiss.

They went and opened the front door. Bear gazed up at the sky and the stars and the moon of the bright new year.

'Honey, look!' said Bear softly.

But he was whispering to himself. Honey was fast asleep. She had closed her eyes, and she did not open them again until the sun came up the next day.

The Mirror

One day, Bear was digging in the garden.
He found something, flat and round and
shiny. Bear lifted it up with his spade.
He took it in his paw and shook off the dirt.

'Honey!' he called. 'Look what I've found!'

Honey flew down onto Bear's shoulder.
She stretched out her neck and looked into
the shiny circle.

'Bear!' she said, 'it's me!'

Bear peered in. 'No it's not, Honey,'
he said. 'It's me.'

Honey and Bear stared at each other,
and at the circle again.

'Bear,' said Honey, 'it's both of us.'

'Except,' said Bear slowly,

'we're backwards.'

Suddenly, Bear felt frightened. He did not want to see himself backwards.

'Put it away, Honey,' he said. 'We don't need it.'

'But it's so useful!' said Honey. 'If I look into it, I can see if a little bit of spaghetti is hanging out of my beak.'

'I could tell you that,' said Bear. 'If you like.'

'It's not the same as seeing it for yourself, Bear,' replied Honey.

Honey was very pleased with what Bear had found in the garden.

She washed it in the sink and dried it in the sun. Then she hung it on a nail just inside the front door.

She looked into it again, with her head on one side. She looked at her eyes and at the silver in her wings.

'I won't look at it, ever!' declared Bear, watching her.

Later that day, Bear passed by the

shiny circle.

He stopped, just for a moment.

He blinked. 'Hello, Bear!' he said, out loud.

Then he ran as fast as he could out the door

and over to the sandpit under the lemon tree.

'Actually,' he said, wriggling his toes in the sand, 'I'm a rather nice-looking Bear!'

Bear's Birthday

It was Bear's birthday.

He was in the garden, standing upside-down on his head.

'Bear,' said Honey, 'what are you doing?'

'Today is my birthday,' said Bear. 'Remember? That means I can do whatever I want. And I want to stand on my head. Look at me!'

Honey looked. She wished she could stand
on her head.

Bear turned the right way up.

'Now I want to do something else,' he said.

'What?' asked Honey.

'Now I want to make a big noise!' said Bear. He pulled out a paper bag suddenly from his pocket.

He blew into the paper bag until it was full of air. Then he popped it – BANG! – with his paw.

'Ow!' said Honey.

'Now I want to play a game,' said Bear. 'Let's play riddles!'

'Oh, good,' said Honey. 'I like riddles.'

'What is big and round and starts with Mmmmmmmmmm?' said Bear.

Honey thought.

'A marble?'

'No,' said Bear.

'A mountain?'

'No,' said Bear.

'Give up?

'A yellow balloon!' Bear laughed and
jumped up and down.

'But Bear –' began Honey, 'that's not . . .'

'It was a tricky riddle, wasn't it?' said Bear.

'Do you want to hear another one?'

'No,' said Honey. She flew away with a
loud flap, high onto the roof.

'Honey?' said Bear, looking up.

'Come down and play with me.'

'I don't want to,' said Honey.

Bear stared. 'Honey,' he said, 'are you crying?'

Honey did not answer.

'It's not very nice of you to cry,' said Bear. 'You are spoiling my birthday.'

Bear sat down on the step. Honey sat up on the roof. They sat and they sat. And they sat. And they sat.

Finally, Bear stood up.

'Honey,' he said, 'would you like to help me blow out the candles on my birthday cake?'

Honey flew down from the roof.

'All right,' she said.

Bear brought out the cake. All the candles were alight.

Bear and Honey blew them out. It took Honey a long time because her breath was so small, but there were no more tears.

Then Bear closed his eyes and made a wish, because it was his birthday, after all.

'What did you wish for, Bear?' asked Honey.

'Just for everything!' said Bear. 'Just everything!'

Bear Gets Lost

Bear was always losing things.

He lost his hat.

He lost his pencils.

He was always losing his socks.

One day, Bear even lost himself.

It was a windy day. Bear loved the wind.

He put on his big blue coat and his scarf and

shouted, 'Goodbye, Honey! I am going out!'

Usually, Honey and Bear went out walking
together. But on this windy day, Bear wanted
to go out by himself.

He walked down to the lake.

He watched the wind pull the water into
waves, and the leaves fly about in the sky.
He opened his mouth and let the air rush
right inside him.

It made him laugh, and he started to run.
He ran up and down with his arms
spread out.

He flopped down and lay still, panting,
with his eyes closed.

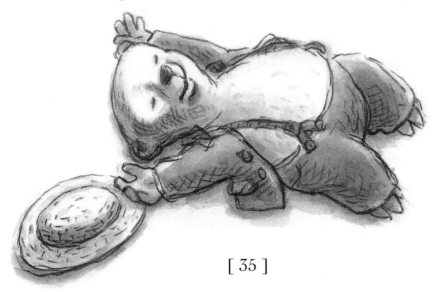

After a while, he sat up and looked about.

He was in a field of grass and flowers,

on top of a slope.

I wonder where I am? he thought.

Am I lost?

Bear rolled himself down the slope like a

rolling pin.

When he came to a stop, he felt dizzy all over. Bear laughed again. I can't be lost, he decided. I don't feel lost. If I were lost, I would feel sad. I would feel lonely. Perhaps I would cry.

But Bear was lost. When it was dark and
he still wasn't home, Honey came looking for
him. She flew far and wide, with a little
lantern around her neck.

At last she found him.

'Bear,' cried Honey, 'There you are!

Did you get lost?'

'I think I did,' said Bear.

Bear was glad that Honey had found him.

He was glad to follow her lantern through

the night all the way back to their home.

But he often thought about the windy day

when he lost himself. It made him feel happy
to remember it.

It was a special day.

Honey's Dream

On Christmas Eve, Honey had the strangest dream.

She dreamed that she was a dove that belonged to a magician.

The magician had a black hat and a big black cape.

When it was time for the magic show to begin, he opened a cage. Honey flew out and perched on his sleeve.

'Abracadabra!' cried the magician.

'I will now make this bird disappear!'

He waved his magic wand. There was a bang
and a cloud of smoke.

Honey was gone!

She found herself on top of a very tall tree.

It was the middle of the night. It was still and silent. There was only one star in the sky. The magician was nowhere to be seen, but Honey could feel magic all around her.

The star grew brighter and shone in Honey's eyes.

What is that sound? she wondered. She heard a rustling, like the beating of hundreds of wings.

She looked down to the ground far below. There were movements in the darkness, of animals and people. The star grew even brighter and a little wind rose.

Honey heard voices singing, then a tiny cry
of something so very small.

'Oh,' Honey whispered, 'I must fly down
and see what it is.'

And she leapt off the tree into the night.

Then Honey woke up. In her own room.
How her heart was thumping!

She stretched out her wings. They were
brown and small, not wide and feathery-
white. She was not a dove on top of a huge
tree. She was Honey.

Bear opened his eyes.

'What is it, Honey?' he asked.

'What's happened?'

'Oh, Bear,' said Honey, flying onto his paw.

'Bear, it's Christmas Day.'